For Simone from Annet

Editor: Kerrie Baldwin
Designer: Paula Winicur
Production Manager: Louise Kurtz

Copyright © 1996 by Esslinger Verlag J. F. Schreiber GmbH,
Esslingen-Wien, Postfach 10 08 25, 73703 Esslingen (Germany)
English-language translation and compilation
copyright © 1999 Abbeville Press.
ISBN 0-7892-0529-7
Story by Nele Moost
Illustrations by Annet Rudolph
Translated by Laura Lindgren

First edition
2 4 6 8 10 9 7 5 3 1

Library of Congress Cataloging-in-Publication Data
Moost, Nele.
It's all mine, or, The little raven's mischief / told by Nele Moost ;
with pictures by Annet Rudolph.
p. cm.
SUMMARY: After tricking the other animals out of their favorite
things, Raven decides that he would rather have friends.
ISBN 0-7892-0529-7
[1. Animals Fiction. 2. Sharing Fiction. 3. Conduct of life Fiction.]
I. Rudolph, Annet, ill. II. Title. III. Title: It's all mine IV. Title: Little
raven's mischief
PZ7.M788175 It 1999
[E]--dc21
99-35466
CIP

IT'S ALL MINE!

or

The Little Raven's Mischief

Story by **Nele Moost**

Illustrations by **Annet Rudolph**

Abbeville Kids

A Division of Abbeville Publishing Group
New York   London

Once upon a time, there was a little raven who didn't have any
friends, because whenever he saw something he liked, he took it,
even if it belonged to someone else. He just couldn't stop himself.
All the other animals had to hide their favorite things, or tie
them down, or lock them away. If they didn't-and sometimes even
if they did-their treasures ended up in Raven's nest high in a tree.

Hedgehog learned his lesson when he left his teddy bear
outside one night. Raven swooped down, and the bear was gone!

After that, the animals were extra careful, but Raven
always thought of new tricks to get what he wanted. . . .

As he watched Raven fly down to him, Wild Pig was determined to keep his brand-new in-line skates. But when Raven met him, they didn't talk about the skates, only about ice cream, chocolate, acorns, and walnuts. Wild Pig started to feel hungry.

Then Raven said, "By the way, if you like acorns, there are some nice ripe ones up that hill." Wild Pig couldn't resist. He pulled off his skates so he could run through the grass and get some acorns. Raven took the abandoned skates.

Owl saw this happen and clutched her gold necklace. She would never fall for such a trick.

But Raven had a new trick in mind. He stood on a limb next to Owl and said, "Wow, what a beautiful gold necklace! It really sparkles, and looks so good on you!"

Owl was flattered, and she said generously, "You can try it on." But, once Raven put on the necklace, off he flew!

"I wouldn't be fooled by such praise," thought Rabbit, who was resting his head on a soft pillow as he watched Owl and Raven above.

Then Raven flew down and pecked at Rabbit with his sharp beak. "If you don't get up right now," Raven cawed, "I'll peck your ears off!"

Rabbit was proud of his long, soft ears, so, to protect them, he ran away, leaving his beloved pillow behind.

Fox laughed at Rabbit's fear. She thought that Raven wouldn't dare to threaten her. Without a worry at all, she wound up her music box and listened to its lovely music. But Raven heard it, too.

Raven
Restricted
Area

MOUSE

No
Trespassing
for
Ravens

Soon Fox went into her den without the music box. Raven then
flew down and loosened a screw on the music box. The music
stopped. When Fox came outside, Raven said, "I think your music
box is broken."

"Let me see it," Fox replied, and she wound it up again. But
no music came out, no matter how much Fox shook it.

"No-good box!" cried Fox as she tossed it away and stomped
into her den. Raven gleefully caught the music box and tightened
the screw.

Sheep had been watching. "He can't break my new red cap,"
she thought.

Raven soon noticed Sheep's new cap and decided to visit her.

"Oh, you're so lucky," he said. "You've got such a nice woolly cap, and you don't even need it. You've got warm, thick fleece all over you, and I'm so cold. I just wish I had something to keep my head warm." Raven shivered pitifully and covered his wings with Sheep's laundry.

"Well," thought Sheep, "he really needs my cap, and I don't need it at all." So she gave the cap to Raven.

Wolf growled to himself, "Begging won't make me give anything away."

Raven noticed that Wolf just received a fantastic new fire engine. But when Raven spoke to him, he said, "Gosh, I didn't know that you still played with toy cars."

"So what if I do?" Wolf muttered.

"Oh, nothing," Raven replied, and hopped a step backwards to be a safe distance away. "I'm just surprised that you still play with baby toys. Aren't you afraid the other animals will laugh at you?"

Suddenly Wolf lost interest in his fire engine and went into his house without it. "Thanks!" said Raven with a sly smile as he quickly snatched his new prize.

Squirrel shook her head. "I don't care what anyone thinks of me!"

Squirrel began practicing her juggling, but the balls kept falling to the ground. Raven was watching and said, "Juggling is very difficult, isn't it? I'll trade with you, if you want to—my new ladder for the balls." Squirrel was pleased and dashed off with the ladder.

Raven was not pleased that he traded away the ladder from his new fire engine, but then he saw Badger reading a thick book.

badgers

Raven decided to visit Badger. He showed him some red wool that he had plucked out of his new cap. "Here," he said to Badger, "I'll share this nice soft wool with you. Will you give me something, too?"

Badger felt embarrassed. He wanted to give Raven something in return.

"O.K.," he finally said. "I've only read half of this book, but you can take it."

Raven happily returned to his nest with the book.

Raven was just starting to read the book when Bear rode by on a tricycle.

"Oh, oh!" cried Raven. Bear stopped and looked up. "Oh! My tooth!" screeched Raven even louder.

"Have you got a toothache?" Bear asked.

"Yes, and it really hurts!" Raven moaned.

"Is there anything I can do?"

"No," whined Raven, "no one can do anything. I'll just try to ignore it."

Bear was about to ride away when he turned to Raven and said, "If you do something that's fun, it will be easier to ignore your toothache. Would you like to ride my tricycle?"

So Raven rode off on the tricycle and didn't return it to Bear.

Raven
lives
here

One day, when Raven was guarding all the treasures in his nest, the animals came to Raven's tree.

Bear called up to him, "We're all going to play make-believe. Will you come and play, too?"

"Sure!" yelled Raven joyfully. It had been such a long time since anyone had asked him to play.

Then Bear said, "And our game would be even more fun if you could bring some toys that we can share."

"Sure!" yelled Raven again, "I have a tricycle to ride, a soft pillow to fall on. . . ." But then Raven remembered that he tricked the animals into giving him these toys. Raven wanted to play with the animals, but he was ashamed of what he had done to such nice friends.

Raven spread his wings over all the toys and said sadly, "I mean, I'll have to look for them, and I still have that awful toothache."

Bear said, "Feel better soon, Raven!" And we'd be happy if you would play with us later!"

The other animals left and played make-believe without him.

The next day the animals played tag together, and the day after that they played hide-and-seek. Raven played alone with the toys in his nest, but he really wanted to join the animals' games.

Raven realized that having friends would make him feel happier than having toys. So he gathered all his toys and took them to where everyone was playing. When Raven reached the animals, he handed the toys back and said, "I am truly sorry."

"It's okay, Raven," said Bear. "We just wanted to play with you."

"We all forgive you," said Hedgehog as he took off his sign warning the animals about the Raven's tricks. "So let's go play make-believe!"

Bear pointed to Snake. "Now everyone has a costume," said Bear, "except Snake."

Raven smiled and said, "He can use my favorite sock!"

They laughed and played all afternoon. And, of course, Snake returned the sock to Raven when the games were over.